CRABTREE SCHOOL

First published in the UK in 2015 by Scholastic Children's Books
An imprint of Scholastic Ltd
Euston House, 24 Eversholt Street
London, NW1 1DB, UK
Registered office: Westfield Road, Southam, Warwickshire, CV47 0RA
SCHOLASTIC and associated logos are trademarks and/or
registered trademarks of Scholastic Inc.

ISBN 978 1407 15327 8

A CIP catalogue record for this book
is available from the British Library

Printed and bound by CPI Group (UK) Ltd, Croydon, CR0 4YY

Papers used by Scholastic Children's Books are made
from wood grown in sustainable forests.

1 3 5 7 9 10 8 6 4 2

www.scholastic.co.uk

CRABTREE SCHOOL

The Case of the Missing Cat

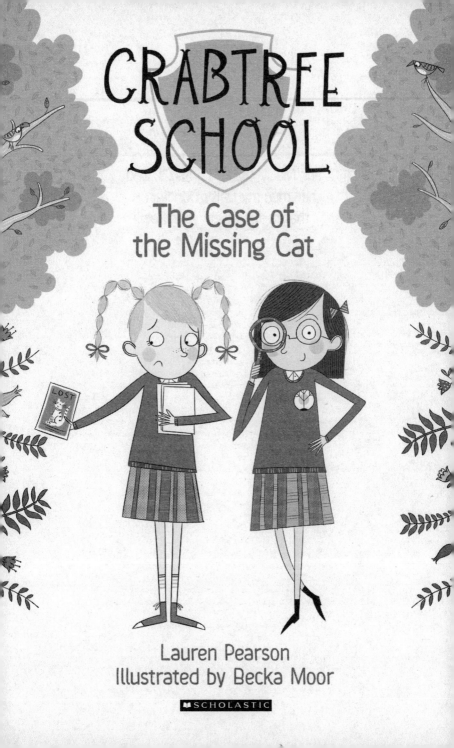

Lauren Pearson
Illustrated by Becka Moor

SCHOLASTIC

For Maisy (AKA "Le Nez"), and
her mummy Daisy Donovan –
thanks for all of your help.

Chapter

A Meow for Help

The whole thing began because of the way Miss Moody went about eating her sweeties.

The Year Three teacher at Crabtree School for Girls always ate the red sweeties out of the pack first. Then she ate the yellow ones, then orange and the blackcurrant last of all. The green ones Miss Moody left in her desk. Her top drawer was full of green sweeties.

Miss Moody was sneaky with her sweeties. She popped them into her mouth between reading out words for spelling tests, or whilst her pupils were getting changed for PE. Miss

Moody ate them when she thought no one was looking, but actually someone *was* looking.

"Miss Moody," said Lottie that morning, as the teacher popped a red sweetie into her mouth after taking the register. "How come you always leave the green ones?"

"Pardon, Lottie?" said Miss Moody in surprise. She swallowed her sweetie without chewing.

"I can't work it out," Lottie told her. "You have a green scarf that you wear nearly every day, so you like green, right, Miss Moody?"

"Yes, Lottie," Miss Moody replied. "I do like green but I don't see how—"

"And you like apples too, because I've seen you eat them," continued Lottie. "Those green sweeties taste like apples. I've had them before."

There was almost nothing going on at Crabtree School that Charlotte "Lottie" Lewis didn't know about. Lottie snooped, she spied and she eavesdropped. She hid behind doors

and crept up on conversations. Lottie knew everything that *had happened* in Crabtree's history, everything that *was happening* at Crabtree right now, and even lots of things that were *about to happen*.

For more than three years, since even before she could write properly, Lottie had filled pages and pages of purple notebooks with all of these happenings. Lottie's current notebook was like a treasure chest of information: you could find out who was friends with whom, and who wasn't, who had been to fun play dates and who hadn't. There were lists of what each year group got up to, maps of the school and the playground, and schedules of what was coming up in the calendar. Even the teachers asked Lottie for information, when they needed it. It was very useful to have her around, most of the time. Unless she happened to be gathering information on *you*.

"Lottie, what on earth—" Miss Moody should have known that Lottie would catch her with her sneaky sweeties, but Lottie had only been in Year Three for a couple of months. Miss Moody had a lot to learn about just how much her nosiest pupil noticed.

"If you like green *and* you like apples," Lottie continued, "then how come you eat sweeties all day, but not the green apple-flavoured ones?"

Ever since they had begun Year Three, Lottie

had been keeping track of Miss Moody's sweetie activity in her notebook, on the page labelled SUBJECT: MISS MOODY. The Case of the Green Sweeties had been driving Lottie mad. Why did Miss Moody not eat the green ones?

SUBJECT: MISS MOODY.

Real Name: RACHEL!!!

Likes to move desks round too often
  why????

Hole in left sleeve of coat.

SNEAKS SWEETS!!!!

Doesn't eat green sweeties—WHY???

~~Doesn't like green?~~

~~Doesn't like apple?~~

Takes No.39 bus to school.

Wears trainers in the morning instead of
  proper teacher shoes!

Age: ~~100?~~ 29.

Friends with Miss Cheeky and

Mr RockanRoll.

Has a photo of her dog on her phone –
FIND OUT NAME.

Always has salad for lunch, no tomatoes.

Home Address: NEED TO FIND THIS
OUT! Follow her?

A hand went up in Year Three.

"Miss Moody," asked Lottie's best friend Isabel from the front row. "Do you really eat sweets *all day*? That's bad for your teeth, you know. My mummy says too many sweets make your teeth turn black and fall out." Isabel couldn't believe that a teacher would do something so unhealthy.

The whole of Year Three leaned forward for a closer look at Miss Moody's teeth.

"No, not *every* day, Isabel," said Miss Moody. "Occasionally, as a small treat, I have one or two sweeties—"

"But, Miss Moody," said Lottie, looking down at her notebook. "Yesterday you had five red ones, three orange ones—"

"LOTTIE! THAT IS QUITE ENOUGH!" said Miss Moody. "Yes, Ava?"

"Miss Moody," said Lottie's friend Ava, who had been waving her hand wildly at the back of the room, "I once heard a story about a boy who ate so many sweeties that the sweetie-making people rang him and said he'd eaten all he was allowed to have for his whole life. He could never have any more of their sweeties ever, ever again for as long as he lived."

"That can't be right," said Zoe from the second row. "But if it is right, then how many sweeties are you allowed in your life? And how could the sweetie company keep track of who ate what sweeties?" There was a murmur as everyone considered this.

"I don't know how many sweeties *that* boy

had," said Lottie. "But Miss Moody has had forty-seven sweets already this month."

"Lottie!" said Miss Moody, turning as red as the sweet she had just eaten. Having Lottie tell the world about her sneaky sweetie habit made Miss Moody embarrassed. "Do me a favour, Lottie, and take this note down to Mrs Peabody's office, please. RIGHT NOW." Miss Moody scribbled a note, folded it in half and handed it to Lottie.

"Don't open it!" said Miss Moody as Lottie went to unfold the note. "Just go!" Lottie heard Isabel telling Miss Moody all about healthy snacks as she closed the classroom door behind her.

Lottie made it down the staircase and through the front hall of Crabtree School without anyone spotting her. Not Being Spotted was an actual game that Lottie played, and she was very good at it. She knew every door to crouch behind, every shadow to hide in and every secret passage to take. (Yes, Crabtree School has secret passages. But they really are *very* secret and can't be described in any further detail. Not yet.)

Because of her exceptional Not Being Spotted skills, Lottie had been at Mrs Biro's side in the school office for some time before the secretary noticed her.

"Goodness gracious, Lottie!" exclaimed Mrs Biro, jumping up from her chair in fright. "How long have you been standing there, dear?"

"Miss Moody gave me a note for you," said Lottie. "It says: 'I thought Lottie could use a little walk'."

Mrs Biro peered down at Lottie through her glasses. "Did Miss Moody give you permission to read that note, Lottie?"

Lottie peered back up at Mrs Biro through her own glasses. "Miss Moody said not to open the note," said Lottie. "And I didn't, I promise. It's just that I could see her writing through the paper."

Mrs Biro frowned.

"Are you going on holiday, Mrs Biro?" asked Lottie. "How come there are loads of pictures of beaches on your computer?" Lottie leaned in for a closer look. "Is that your daughter on the beach? Is that your grandson? How old is he? What is his name?"

"Oh," said Mrs Biro, going a bit red. "Oh, that. Yes. . . Shouldn't you go back to class now, Lottie?" Mrs Biro clicked her mouse and the beaches were gone.

"What's this?" Lottie asked Mrs Biro, forgetting about the beach and pointing to a note stuck on the secretary's desk. Lottie struggled to read the secretary's handwriting. "Does this say nits? Does someone in Year One have nits?! Who is it?" Lottie reached for her notebook.

"Lottie!" Mrs Biro was about to talk to Lottie about minding your own business (a talk that the secretary had given Lottie many times before) when there was a noise from the room next door. It sounded like a cat crying for help.

When they went to investigate, Mrs Biro and Lottie saw something very strange: the headmistress of Crabtree School for Girls was crawling around on the floor of her office. Mrs Peabody was peering under the furniture and making kissing noises. Then she stopped and meowed. She shook something in her hand that made a jingling noise.

"Mrs Peabody?" said Lottie and Mrs Biro together.

"Oh, we must *do* something!" cried Mrs Peabody, looking up at them. Lottie could see

that the headmistress was holding a toy mouse with a bell on it. "I haven't seen hide nor hair of Lady Lovelypaws in four days! She won't even come out to play with her favourite mousie."

The headmistress meowed a few more times. Lottie had seen her do this before, and usually Lady Lovelypaws, the official cat of Crabtree School, came running. It was as if the cat and the headmistress spoke the same language. But today Lady Lovelypaws did not appear.

"You see?" sobbed Mrs Peabody. "Nothing! Lady Lovelypaws is gone! She has vanished!"

If it hadn't been for her investigation into the green sweeties, Lottie would never have been sent down to the office that day. Which would have meant that Lottie wouldn't have been there with Mrs Biro to hear Mrs Peabody's meow for help.

But as it happened, Lottie landed herself right at the centre of a true-life, for-real, missing-cat mystery.

Chapter

Oi! Have You Seen this Cat?

Lady Lovelypaws had vanished into thin air. As soon as Mrs Peabody declared the cat missing, Lottie helped to organize a school-wide search. They checked all of Lady Lovelypaws's favourite places. She was not snoozing in the paper tray on Mrs Peabody's desk. She was not perched on the high landing at the top of the staircase, watching the goings-on in the front hallway. She was not curled up in one of the fuzzy beanbag chairs in the Rainbow Room, waiting for the Crabtree girls to come into the best room in the school to hear a visiting author or watch a movie.

Each year group checked their classroom from floor to ceiling. Every girl, from Reception to Year Six, looked under every desk and in every cubbyhole. Lottie watched Year Three as they dug through the smelly socks in their PE kits and rummaged through the bits of paper and old spelling tests in their school bags. No one found so much as a whisker.

Colonel Crunch, who was the school groundskeeper, scoured the playground. He looked at the top of the slide, in the tree house and amongst the flowers that lined the playground. He climbed the famous crab apple trees and peeked around in

the branches. All he found were a few old chewed-up toy mice and a nest full of very cross birds.

Colonel Crunch rummaged around in his tool shed, searched the area where the scooters were kept, and checked the garden patch where the Green Thumb Club grew vegetables for school meals. But it was all for nothing.

Mrs Crunch, who was the school dinner

lady and Colonel Crunch's wife, emptied the cupboards in the school kitchen. She looked in every sack of flour and in every basket of apples waiting to be made into her famous crumble. Together, the Crunches even searched the cottage where they lived next door to the school, thinking that perhaps Lady Lovelypaws had fancied a bit of a wander. She was not there either.

The music teacher, Mr Rockanroll, did not find Lady Lovelypaws hiding under the drum set, nor under the lid of his piano. Mrs Potion did not uncover her in the science lab, nor did Mrs Method, the drama teacher, find her backstage amongst the scenery and costumes.

By the end of the day, Lottie's friends in Year Three were beginning to give up hope.

"Maybe," said Ava, "aliens came and took her. Or fairies. Or ghosts." Ava had the craziest imagination of anyone that Lottie knew.

"This is a true-life investigation," said Lottie. "What we need are CLUES and, except for the toy mice, there aren't any."

"I wonder," said Isabel helpfully, "if we should

try to work out who saw Lady Lovelypaws last?"

That was a good idea. Lottie wished that she had thought of it first.

"How will we do that?" asked Zoe, who was a bit dusty from searching the floor underneath their coat hooks. "Counting the teachers and every student, we would have to ask..." Zoe did a bit of thinking. "One hundred and seventy-one people when they last saw Lady Lovelypaws." Zoe loved maths, especially when it could be used in real life.

"Hmmm..." said Lottie, tapping her chin with her index finger. "That would take ages. It's nearly going-home time."

"Sometimes, at mine, we write notes to each other," said their friend Rani. Rani had four brothers, so her house was like a small school. A small boys' school. Even though Rani was the new girl and had only just joined their class, she loved Crabtree School more than any of them, partly because it had no boys.

"When something goes missing at my house," Rani went on, "one of my brothers will leave a note by the door that says, 'Oi! Has anyone seen my football boots?'"

"That's a good idea," agreed Lottie. "Let's make a missing person poster! We can ask if anyone has seen Lady Lovelypaws since last week!"

"You mean a missing *cat* poster," corrected Isabel.

Lottie, Isabel, Zoe, Rani and Ava hurried off to see Ms Mess in the art room. "Oi! Has anyone seen this cat?" didn't sound quite right, but in no time they had come up with this instead:

MISSING

HAVE YOU SEEN THIS CAT?

NAME: LADY LOVELYPAWS, CRABTREE SCHOOL CAT

LAST SEEN BY MRS PEABODY NEAR THE KITCHEN LAST WEDNESDAY MORNING HAVING HER FOOD

PEOPLE WITH ANY CLUES SHOULD TELL LOTTIE, AVA, ISABEL, RANI OR ZOE OR MRS PEABODY

IF YOU HAVE SEEN HER SINCE LAST WEEK, PLEASE TELL US

HER LIFE DEPENDS ON IT!

"Do you really think her life depends on it?" asked Ava fearfully as Lottie added the last bit.

"Yes!" declared Lottie. "Lady Lovelypaws could be in real, true-life danger. She could be trapped in a big hole and she can't jump out. She could be lost, and not know her way home. We have to find her!"

The friends decided to make lots of posters. Isabel, who was very good at crafts, drew a picture of Lady Lovelypaws at the bottom of each one. Then she added some glitter. Lottie wasn't sure about the glitter, but Isabel thought that the prettier the poster was, the more people would look at it.

Once they'd finished the posters, the girls put them up all around Crabtree School. Isabel was president of the Crabtree School Jolly Neighbourhood Helpers Club, and she promised to get the club members to tape a few posters up in Crabtree Park across the street. Perhaps someone might have found Lady Lovelypaws there, and not known where to return her.

Lady Lovelypaws's glittery face was everywhere by the time the bell rang for home time.

Chapter

SCAT!

The Case of the Missing Cat took a worrying turn the next day. No one came forward as having seen Lady Lovelypaws after cat breakfast time last Wednesday. But someone *had* seen her photo on the posters in the park. This someone was concerned about Lady Lovelypaws for all the wrong reasons.

Just before morning break time, Lottie had come down the stairs to find a strange woman in the front hall. This woman was standing in front of the big statue of Lady Constance Hawthorne, Crabtree School's very first headmistress. The funny thing was, the statue looked more alive than the real-life lady. This visitor had a most peculiar face. It was smooth and perfectly still, like someone had made it out of clay.

What Lottie didn't know was that the visitor's face was frozen because she never smiled or laughed. Never, ever. In fact, she usually did just the opposite: when she wasn't talking, the sides of the mysterious visitor's mouth curved down ever so slightly, like she had just tasted something rotten.

Lottie had been so caught up in staring at this living statue that she hadn't noticed what was in the woman's hand; she was carrying one of their missing cat posters! Did this mean that she had found Lady Lovelypaws?

As Mrs Biro took the visitor's long grey coat, Lottie dashed behind their backs into the headmistress's office. She dived under one of the chairs opposite Mrs Peabody's desk whilst the headmistress was having a sip of her tea. For someone as good at Not Being Spotted as Lottie was, it wasn't a very good hiding place. Luckily, Mrs Peabody didn't have time to notice because the visitor barged right in behind Lottie.

The stranger did not waste time with hellos. "My name," said the woman to Mrs Peabody coldly, "is Mrs Bethel Snoop."

"Mrs Penelope Peabody," said Mrs Peabody. "A pleasure to meet you. Welcome to Crabtree School."

"Mrs Peabody," said Mrs Snoop. "I can see from these posters in Crabtree Park that you are keeping a CAT in Crabtree School for Girls, is that right?"

Lottie could see Ava, Zoe, Rani and Isabel outside the headmistress's open window, peering into the office. Her friends must have seen the visitor coming too. They were all staring at the stranger's stony face.

"Yes," replied Mrs Peabody to Mrs Snoop, "Lady Lovelypaws is our school cat. But as you can see ..." the headmistress pointed to the flier in Mrs Snoop's hand, "she's gone missing. It's dreadful. We are heartbroken. Have you seen her?"

"What is dreadful, Mrs Peabody," said Mrs Snoop, ignoring the headmistress's question, "is that this feline was ever allowed on school grounds in the first place!"

"I beg your pardon?" said Mrs Peabody.

"I am the president of the Society for the Containment of Animal Tolerance," said Mrs Snoop. "Otherwise known as SCAT."

"Sorry?" said Mrs Peabody again. "I don't understand."

Lottie wiggled her notebook out of her pocket and wrote SCAT on a blank page.

"We at SCAT believe that animals do not

belong anywhere near children. They certainly should not be in schools," said Mrs Snoop. "Animals are filthy, vicious creatures that give children germs and allergies."

"What is she saying?" Lottie heard Rani whisper to Ava. "And look how can she talk without moving her lips!" It was true. Mrs Snoop's mouth was perfectly still, even when she was speaking.

"She's saying that Lady Lovelypaws is mean and dirty!" explained Ava. "And that she might make us sneeze!"

From her position on the floor Lottie could see the framed photo of Lady Lovelypaws that Mrs Peabody kept on her desk. In the picture, Lady Lovelypaws's white fur was glorious and fluffy and her lips were curled into a warm smile. Lady Lovelypaws really could smile; she was a most extraordinary cat. She certainly wasn't filthy *or* vicious.

"Ah, yes," said Mrs Peabody. "I seem to remember getting a letter from SCAT earlier this term after our student Charlotte Lewis brought her dog, Pip, in for the day." Mrs Peabody glanced down at Lottie under the chair. "You don't approve of pets visiting schools, then, Mrs Snoop?"

"Having a pet *visit* is bad enough," said Mrs Snoop. "I'm happy to report that we have nearly put an end to pet school visits throughout this fine city."

No more pet visits sounded terrible to Lottie. Every spring, Crabtree School held a Bring Your Pet to School Parade. Would they not be allowed this any more? Lottie's dog, Pip, would be so disappointed! And that wasn't even the worst of it.

"To have a cat *living* in a school is against everything that we at SCAT stand for," continued Mrs Snoop. "AND it is also against rule four thousand, three hundred and twenty-one of the Official Rules for All Primary Schools Everywhere. The rule clearly says NO ANIMALS."

"But we've had a cat here at Crabtree School for hundreds of years," said Mrs Peabody. "And we've never had a problem."

Mrs Peabody was talking about all the cats that had lived at Crabtree School before Lady Lovelypaws had even been born. But Lottie misunderstood the headmistress.

"Lady Lovelypaws is A HUNDRED YEARS OLD?" she cried out. Lottie forgot that she was supposed to be hiding, which almost never happened.

Mrs Snoop was none too pleased to find a child under her chair, although her face of stone didn't show it.

"Up at once!" she told Lottie, without changing her expression. "Get up this very minute! Just think of how dirty that floor is if there is a CAT about."

"But there *isn't* a cat about," called Zoe from outside the window. "That's the problem!"

"No," Mrs Snoop told them. "That is not a problem at all. Because if I hear that a cat is back on these school grounds, I shall be forced to call the mayor to report the violation of rule four thousand, three hundred and twenty-one and arrange for the removal of the offending feline."

"What did she say?" Ava asked Isabel.

"She said that she is going to take Lady Lovelypaws away if we ever find her!" replied Isabel.

"You can't take our cat away," said Mrs Peabody firmly to Mrs Snoop. "She's lived here for years, and her mother and grandmother and great-grandmother all lived here before her. I love her, the girls love her—"

"Lady Lovelypaws looks after us," Rani told Mrs Snoop. "When you are feeling sad at school, Lady Lovelypaws comes and cuddles you."

"Dis*gus*ting!" declared Mrs Snoop, looking at Rani in horror. "Cats are horrid animals that do not belong near small children. NO MORE CUDDLING WITH CATS! We must find this vile creature and hand it over to SCAT. ASAP."

"What's ASAP?" Rani asked Zoe. "Is that like SCAT?"

"It means 'As Soon As Possible'," Lottie said, coming to stand by the window as Mrs Snoop marched out of Mrs Peabody's office. "And it means that we need to find Lady Lovelypaws ASAP, too."

"But if we find her, SCAT will take her away!" said Rani, her eyes full of tears. Lady Lovelypaws had been very kind and welcoming when Rani was brand new at Crabtree School. Rani loved her like she was her very own cat.

Lottie climbed out of the window to give Rani a hug, but the tears still came.

It was known throughout the world that Mrs Peabody could not bear to see a child cry. Rani's sobs made huge red hives appear on Mrs Peabody's face. Smoke swirled from the headmistress's nose and her knees began to knock together.

"Just find her," said Mrs Peabody to the five friends outside her window. "Find her before Mrs Snoop does!"

Chapter

A Break in the Case

Mrs Snoop's threat to take Lady Lovelypaws away made the search for the Crabtree cat even more important. They had to find Lady Lovelypaws before SCAT did.

After lunch, two things happened that brought the friends new hope.

"That's so very odd," said a puzzled Mrs Peabody to Lottie in the hallway by the kitchen. "Last night, I'm sure there was some food left in Lady Lovelypaws's bowl. Now this morning, it's gone." Mrs Peabody looked sadly down at the empty cat bowl.

Lottie knew a clue when she found one.
She wrote:

MISSING CAT FOOD?

down in her notebook.

Then, on their way out to the playground,
Lottie and her friends found Colonel Crunch by
the flowerbeds. The groundskeeper was staring at
the ground, and scratching his head.

"What is it?" said Lottie. She thought about
the note she'd seen on Mrs Biro's desk. "Have
you got the nits from someone in Year One,
Colonel Crunch?"

"Certainly not!" barked the Colonel. "It's just
that, I swear I left Lady Lovelypaws's toy mice
on the pavement by the kitchen door yesterday.
Then this morning I found them here in the
flowers."

Mice on the move was definitely a clue.

Two clues together gave Lottie an idea.

"This is the biggest bowl of cat food I've ever seen!" said Rani. "It could feed Lady Lovelypaws for a week!"

"I've marked how full the bowl is, here," said Lottie, pointing to a line drawn in black marker on the inside of Lady Lovelypaws's dish. "So we'll be able to tell if she eats any."

"What if something else eats it?" asked Ava. "Like a fairy or an alien?"

"Or a squirrel smart enough to use the cat flap," added Isabel.

"I'm pretty sure squirrels sleep at night," replied Lottie. "The clues were all found in the morning. If we leave this bowl out when we go home, we should be able to tell if Lady Lovelypaws comes out after we are gone to eat the food. If she does, it means that she is here in the school somewhere, hiding!"

"Why would she do that?" asked Zoe.

No one knew, but the next morning, they

discovered proper proof that Lady Lovelypaws *was* hiding in Crabtree School, and also proof that she was hungry: the food in the bowl was nearly all gone.

"It could have been a fox," said Colonel Crunch uneasily. He didn't like the idea of foxes in his school at night.

"No," said Lottie. "It WAS Lady Lovelypaws! Look!" They all gasped as, between two fingers, Lottie held up a real and true clue: a white cat hair.

"It was next to the bowl," explained Lottie.

"It's her! It's really her!" shrieked Mrs Peabody, seizing the cat hair. She and Colonel Crunch raced off to begin searching anew.

"I really don't understand," said Zoe, when the friends were alone in the hallway. "Why would Lady Lovelypaws hide from us? Why would she disappear all day and only come out at night?"

"I don't know," said Lottie. "But I know how we can find out."

"How?" asked Zoe, Isabel, Ava and Rani, all at the same time. Lottie looked deadly serious. They leaned in close to listen: whatever this plan was, it was going to be big.

"We are going to SPEND THE NIGHT IN CRABTREE SCHOOL!"

Convincing Mrs Peabody that they needed to have a sleepover in Crabtree School was easier than Lottie might have thought. The headmistress was desperate to find her deputy-head cat. Every time Mrs Peabody looked out of her office window, Mrs Snoop just happened to be strolling by the school, her stony eyes searching for cat hiding places. In the end Mrs Peabody even agreed to stay over *with* Lottie and her friends, because of course they would need a grown-up to order the pizzas.

"Pizzas?" asked Mrs Peabody.

"Yes," said Ava. "Even though we're solving a mystery, it still has to be a proper sleepover! Pizzas, ghost stories, popcorn. . ."

"And most importantly, finding Lady Lovelypaws!" Lottie reassured the bewildered headmistress.

🌳

Lottie's mum took more persuading than Mrs Peabody.

"But, Lottie," she said as they walked home from school, "you've only ever been to sleepovers at Gran's! Won't you be scared?"

"Of course not!" Lottie told her. "I'll be too busy to be scared. Besides, Ava and Isabel and Zoe and Rani will be with me. And Mrs Peabody."

"A sleepover at *school*?" Lottie's mum said. "Whoever heard of a sleepover at school?" They stopped for a minute to let Pip catch up. Pip was their dog, and he was nearly one thousand years old in dog years.

"Can I have a sleepover at school, too?" asked Lola, Lottie's little sister.

"Reception girls are too little to have sleepovers," Lottie told her. "You'd be crying for Mummy even before tea! Besides, Mrs Peabody gave special permission just for me and my friends." That last bit was true; for though Mrs Peabody loved each and every Crabtree girl, there was a special place in her heart for Lottie, Ava, Zoe, Isabel and Rani. The friends had been through all sorts of adventures together, and the headmistress knew that if anyone could save the day, they could.

Lottie and her family started for home again, with Pip trudging along behind them. "Lottie, Dad and I could not be popping out to get you in the middle of the night," Lottie's mum said sternly. "Where would you sleep, anyway?"

"We have already made a plan," said Lottie excitedly. "We are going to set up a tent in the front hall!"

Missing a chance to spend the night in a tent was too much for Lola. "That's not fair!!!" she said. "You're mean, Lottie! I'm big enough for a sleepover! I'm almost five!" Lola started to cry. She refused to walk any further, and Pip took the opportunity to lie down on the pavement. He began to snore as Lola howled.

Whilst her mum got crosser and crosser, Lottie resorted to begging. "Please, Mummy, please," she said. "A trillion times please? Googolplex pleases?" Googolplex was the largest number ever; Zoe was always going on about it. (Probably right now Zoe was saying googolplex pleases to her mummy too.)

Whether it was the googolplex pleases or the fact that Lottie's mum wanted to get home before midnight, she finally gave in and said that Lottie could go.

"I'm still worried you'll change your mind in the middle of the night," Lottie's mum said. "Maybe one of us should go with you? The trouble is, Dad's back is hurting and I don't really fancy sleeping on the floor. Hmmm. Maybe Lola could actually—"

Lottie and her mum both looked down at Lola, who was rolling about on the ground. She was holding her breath because she hadn't got her way, and she was turning blue. Taking Lola on the sleepover was out of the question.

Then a snore from her feet gave Lottie an idea. "I'll take Pip!" she said. "Pip can help us find Lady Lovelypaws!"

Lottie knelt down on the pavement, lifted up one of Pip's floppy ears and spoke softly to him. "Pip, do you want to come on a sleepover with me? We can tell ghost stories and look for Lady Lovelypaws?"

Pip opened one eye and looked at Lottie. Lottie watched as his tail moved one tiny centimetre to the left, and then one tiny centimetre to the right.

Pip had agreed to attend the sleepover.

After a minute the dog's heavy eyelid drooped closed again. He began to snore even more loudly than before.

"Well," said Lottie's mum, "he'll be very good at the sleeping bit!"

Chapter

Everything but the Kitchen Sink

Everyone knows that planning for a sleepover is almost as much fun as actually going to one. Lottie and her friends couldn't have the sleepover on a school night, so they had to wait two whole days for it to be Friday. In the meantime, Lottie tried to carry on with her normal activities. At home, she spied on the neighbours like she always did, and wrote down what her parents watched on television at night, who they spoke to on the phone and what they ate for breakfast. At school, Lottie continued her tally of Miss Moody's sweeties. She played loads of rounds of Not Being Spotted, and she found out Year Three's homework before Miss Moody even assigned it. Lottie also kept count of how many times she saw Mrs Snoop walking by Crabtree School. That number was getting worryingly high.

Mostly though, Lottie planned for the sleepover. Her notebook was filled with pages and pages of suggested sleepover plans, lists of things she wanted to bring with her, and even a diagram of exactly how they should sleep so that they would all fit in the tent.

What was truly exciting was that all of the sleepover plans had to be kept secret. Mrs Peabody had agreed to let Ava, Zoe, Rani, Isabel and Lottie spend the night at Crabtree School, but she couldn't very well invite the rest of the school to join them. A sleepover of that size would be a nightmare to organize. Also, if they were going to coax Lady Lovelypaws to come out of hiding, they couldn't have too many people around. But they didn't want to hurt anyone's feelings, or have any more tantrums like Lola's, so they had to keep their plans to themselves. This meant whispering.

"We have to tell ghost stories," whispered Ava during PE on the Thursday. "Every sleepover has ghost stories." Ava and Zoe had already had three sleepovers and there had been ghost stories at every one.

"Not the really scary ones!" whispered Zoe. Thanks to Ava's crazy imagination, Zoe had to check inside her cupboard and under her bed every night before she went to sleep.

During break time on Thursday afternoon, Rani whispered to them about the midnight feasts her older brothers had when they went to sleepovers. "When it gets very dark and very late," Rani looked round to make sure no one else was listening, "we have to go to the kitchen and sneak loads of food. Especially sweeties and cakes."

Isabel thought that they would have to have a midnight tooth-brushing session, too. She didn't want their teeth turning black and falling out, like Miss Moody's were going to.

After lunch on Friday, Isabel and Lottie sat in the tree house writing up the final sleepover plan whilst the other three stayed below, chasing away anyone who came near the ladder.

When they were finished with the final, official sleepover plan, it looked like this:

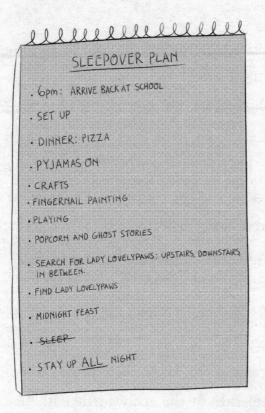

SLEEPOVER PLAN

- 6pm: ARRIVE BACK AT SCHOOL
- SET UP
- DINNER: PIZZA
- PYJAMAS ON
- CRAFTS
- FINGERNAIL PAINTING
- PLAYING
- POPCORN AND GHOST STORIES
- SEARCH FOR LADY LOVELYPAWS: UPSTAIRS, DOWNSTAIRS IN BETWEEN.
- FIND LADY LOVELYPAWS
- MIDNIGHT FEAST
- ~~SLEEP~~
- STAY UP ALL NIGHT

Miss Moody kindly made photocopies of the schedule for each of the five friends, for the Year Three teacher was in on the sleepover plan too. She had even agreed to stay the night to give Mrs Peabody some grown-up company.

It was a very strange thing to arrive at school

49

at teatime. Lottie felt nervous as she tugged at Pip's lead.

"My goodness, Lottie, that is a big bag for just one night!" said Mrs Peabody, as she opened the front door. With her dad's help, Lottie wheeled her giant suitcase through the hallway as Pip trudged along behind her.

"Is Pip staying?" asked Mrs Peabody. "Won't he chase Lady Lovelypaws away?"

Mrs Peabody, Lottie and Lottie's dad all stared at Pip. The old dog had stopped under the giant statue of Lady Hawthorne. Pip looked to one side of the hallway, then to the other. He sniffed the air. He lay down, rolled over on to his back and began to snore.

"Pip doesn't do much chasing," Lottie's dad explained. "Mostly he does sleeping. We thought he might keep you all company."

"Ah yes, of course," said Mrs Peabody. "But does he like cats?"

"Of course he does. And Pip is a dog detective, aren't you, Pip?" said Lottie, stroking his head. "Pip always *looks* like he is sleeping," Lottie told Mrs Peabody. "So you forget that he is there. But secretly, he's watching everything. He has come to help us find Lady Lovelypaws!"

The dog detective did not move when Lottie's dad said goodbye and goodnight, nor did he open his eyes when, one by one, the other slumber party guests arrived.

When all the parents had finished their "be good!" speeches and were gone, Lottie looked around the big front hallway for the best place to set up the tent.

"Here!" she said, pointing right next to the statue of Lady Hawthorne. "We'll put the tent here, facing the front door." Lottie opened her ginormous suitcase. She took out a huge tent and loads of tent poles.

The friends had played with the tent so many

times in Lottie's garden that they put it up in seconds. Mrs Peabody watched in amazement as each girl took out a sleeping bag and began unrolling it inside the expertly assembled tent.

"I hope you don't mind, girls," the headmistress said, "but Miss Moody and I are going to sleep in my office. I've never been very fond of tents – and I must tell you that I prefer cats to dogs," she added nervously, watching Lottie unpack Pip's dog bed and put it next to her sleeping bag.

Mrs Peabody went to find Miss Moody whilst the preparations continued. Isabel reached into her flowery overnight bag and pulled out a big quilt, which she spread out on the floor in front of the tent. Then she took out some bunting and began to hang it around their campsite. She had also made a sign for the side of the tent that read DETECTIVES SLEEPING on one side and DETECTIVES AWAKE on the other.

Ava unpacked a pile of books and a whole

load of dolls from her purple rucksack and laid them out on the quilt. She had brought five dolls, one for each of them, and pyjamas and a change of clothes for each doll. The dolls even had their *own* little tent, with sleeping bags and tiny pillows.

Zoe had a stack of board games and some glow-in-the-dark stickers to put on the ceiling of the tent. "This way, it's like we are sleeping outside, but without the wild animals and bugs," she explained.

Rani had brought nail polish and was proudly setting it out next to the quilt. She had special glitter that went on top of the polish and a small battery-powered fan to make it dry faster.

Soon they had a proper, cosy campsite full of sleepovery things to do.

Lottie waited until her friends had finished unpacking before reaching back into her own suitcase. Then, as Rani, Zoe, Ava and Isabel looked on, Lottie took out five torches, an ancient camera, two pieces of rope, four tins of cat food, a magnifying glass, a compass, three new toy mice filled with catnip, five water bottles, the photocopied sleepover plans and a stack of envelopes.

Lottie had not forgotten the real reason for the sleepover. She arranged all of her supplies on the quilt.

"What is the rope for?" asked Rani.

"In case we need to tie up a baddie," said Lottie. "Or Lady Lovelypaws, if she keeps on running away. And the envelopes are in case we find clues."

They were dividing up the torches when Mrs Peabody and Miss Moody appeared with big boxes of pizza.

"Let me just pop into the kitchen and get some plates," said Mrs Peabody, but it turned out that there was no need: Lottie went to her suitcase and returned with paper plates, serviettes and plastic cutlery, although only Isabel and the grown-ups wanted knives and forks.

They had a pizza picnic on the quilt as the sun went down behind the playground trees. Colonel and Mrs Crunch appeared with a big tray of apple crumble for pudding. The dark school loomed large around them as the night set in, and the halls echoed with teatime chatter and the sound of giggling.

Chapter

The Little Kitten of Death

After dinner was finished and tidied away, and the Crunches had gone home to watch the evening news, it was time to get ready for bed. Even if bedtime was hours and hours away.

"Lottie, are those your pyjamas?" asked Ava, as they finished getting changed.

Lottie stood before them in black leggings, a black T-shirt and black plimsolls. She had a black cap on her head. The other four could hardly see her in the darkness of the hallway.

"Those are strange pyjamas," agreed Isabel,

turning a torch on Lottie. "You look like a burglar."

"They aren't pyjamas," said Lottie. "This is what you wear to solve a mystery at night."

"Oh," said the other four together.

There was an awkward silence as Lottie looked around at her friends.

Isabel had brought pink flannel pyjamas with a matching robe and bunny slippers. Lottie frowned. Surely people solving a mystery didn't wear fuzzy animals on their feet?

Ava was wearing a long white nightdress that nearly touched the floor. Lottie had never seen a detective who looked so much like a fairy-tale princess. This was not good.

Zoe had pyjamas with glow-in-the-dark stars on them. They were so bright that Zoe wouldn't need a torch at all. So much for sneaking up on Lady Lovelypaws. *At least*, thought Lottie, *they would be able to find Zoe in the dark.*

Lottie had expected Rani to have some sensible, handed-down boy-pyjamas from her brothers, but that was not the case. Rani had on sparkly pink trousers and a top with a glittery unicorn jumping over a rainbow. She looked more ready for a disco than for solving a mystery. Lottie *was* pleased to see that Rani had put her trainers back on: at least one of them was prepared to chase Lady Lovelypaws if the investigation called for it.

"Are you in your pyjamas, girls?" asked Mrs

Peabody. She had emerged from her office wearing her nightdress and robe, and fuzzy slippers that looked like the bunny parents of Isabel's slippers. Mrs Peabody had curlers in her hair. Behind her, Miss Moody wore green pyjamas with sheep on them and thick socks on her feet.

"Shall we have a look for Lady Lovelypaws now?" the headmistress asked.

Lottie took out the official sleepover schedule. "It is too early for that," she told them. "It's time for ghost stories and popcorn!"

"You get started with the stories," Miss Moody told them. "Mrs Peabody and I will get the popcorn going." The teacher and the headmistress went off to the Rainbow Room, which held Crabtree School's very own popcorn-making machine, just like the ones they have at the cinema.

"Do we have to have ghost stories?" asked

Zoe, looking nervously at Ava. "Maybe we could skip that bit."

"Of course we have to have ghost stories," said Lottie. "It's all written down right here." She waved the sleepover schedule about.

"It's awfully dark in here," said Rani. "Why don't we turn some more lights on and *then* tell ghost stories?"

"That's what the TORCHES are for, silly!" said Ava. "You need darkness for ghost stories, and then the torches make it even spookier."

"We'll waste the batteries," said Zoe hopefully. "And we need the torches for later, when we look for Lady Lovelypaws. Oh well, I guess no ghost stories." Zoe sounded delighted.

"Don't worry," said Lottie, taking five packets of extra batteries out of her suitcase. "I've already thought of that."

There didn't seem to be any other reason why they couldn't have ghost stories, and so

Ava, a torch lighting up her face, began.

"This story," she said chillingly, "is called 'The Little Kitten of Death'."

"Stop!" screeched Zoe. "I already don't like this one."

"It's not that scary," said Ava. "But how about I call it, 'The Little Ghost Kitten' instead?"

Zoe didn't look convinced, but Ava continued.

"A long, long time ago, in a big red school just like this one, in fact it was *this one, there was a little girl called Mabel. Mabel loved her friends and her school and her very kind headmistress, who was called Lady Constance Hawthorne, just like the statue says.*

"One night, Mabel was alone in this very hallway after an evening music lesson when she felt a tug at the back of her dress.

"Now this was the olden days, so Mabel wore long skirts with lots of lace. She thought she might have got her dress caught on something. But when

she turned round, there was nothing there.

"She kept walking, but there it was again – Tug! Tug!"

In the darkness, Ava tugged on Zoe's foot. Zoe screamed and smacked Ava's hand. Rani pulled the quilt up over her head, whilst Isabel looked nervously round the dark hallway.

Only Lottie was not afraid. "Go on!" she told Ava. "Was it a ghost?"

Ava did go on, in her spookiest voice.

"Mabel turned again and, this time, she saw a fluffy white kitten near her shoe. She bent down to pick it up, but her hands went right through it!

"Suddenly, the kitten turned and ran up the stairs. Mabel knew that it was a ghost, but she was not afraid."

"I am!" shrieked Zoe.

"It's not THAT scary," Lottie told Zoe crossly. "It's only a kitten. A ghost *kitten* isn't scary."

Lottie probably should not have said that,

because then Ava decided to make the story even scarier.

"*Because she wasn't a scaredy cat like Zoe, Mabel decided to follow the kitten. As she climbed the stairs — those very stairs right there — Mabel could hear a voice calling out: 'Here, kitty-kitty-kitty. . . Here, kitty-kitty-kitty. . .'*

"*It was quiet at first, but as Mabel got closer to the Year Three classroom, the voice got louder. The classroom door was closed, and the kitten disappeared right through it.*

"*'Here, kitty-kitty-kitty,' called the voice.*

"*Mabel knew that the girls in her class had all gone home. She couldn't imagine who could have been calling out, 'Here, kitty-kitty,' over and over again. . .*

"*Then there was a scratching on the bottom of the door, like the kitten wanted to get back out.*"

Ava scratched her fingers on the floor and they all jumped, even Lottie.

"Mabel was very, very scared but she had to know who was in there.

" 'Here, kitty-kitty-kitty. . .' went the voice. Mabel put her hand on the doorknob, and slowly, slowly she began to turn it, and—

"'BOOOOOOO!'"

"AHHHHHH!" screamed Zoe, as Rani pulled at the quilt so hard that it toppled their camp. Nail polish and dolls went everywhere. Even Pip raised his head to see what all the commotion was about.

"Oh no!" shrieked Isabel. "Look, the popcorn!"

Miss Moody and Mrs Peabody had been on their way back to the hall with two huge bowls of popcorn, all that was left in the popcorn maker. The end of the ghost story and all the screaming had given them such a fright that they had dropped the popcorn all over the floor.

"I told you," Zoe told Ava crossly as they

scooped up dusty popcorn, "not to make it too scary! Now you've ruined our popcorn party."

"I'm sorry," said Ava. "I was only having fun. I never meant to hurt the popcorn. I just wanted to tell a good story."

"It *was* a good story," Lottie told her. "But what happened at the end?"

"What do you mean?" asked Ava. "I said 'Boo'. That was the end."

"But we have to know what happens," said Lottie. "You can't just end with Boo! Who was the voice? The voice behind the door?"

"Oh," said Ava. "It was the ghost of Lady Constance Hawthorne, of course, calling out for Lady Lovelypaws's great-great-great-great grandmother."

Lottie nodded approvingly.

"That was way too scary," said Zoe. "In my head I can still hear her calling, 'Here, kitty, kitty!'" Zoe shivered in fear.

"Wait, listen!" cried Rani. "I hear it too!"

They all froze. Then suddenly Lottie ran to the front door. When she threw it open, she found Mrs Snoop on the front path.

"Just passing by," Mrs Snoop said calmly, heading off down the street and calling "Here, kitty, kitty", as she went.

"She was calling for Lady Lovelypaws," said Rani. "She's trying to catch her before we can!"

"Mrs Snoop is even scarier than the ghost story!" said Zoe, and her friends agreed.

* * *

"Maybe," Isabel suggested as they scooped the last bit of popcorn into a bin, "we could string up this dirty popcorn and use it to decorate the tent? Like you do on a Christmas tree?"

It was indeed crafts time on the sleepover schedule. The girls tidied the campsite and made Isabel's popcorn chains. Then Rani painted everyone's toenails. Once they were dry, the friends put Ava's dolls into their pyjamas and tucked them into bed in their little tent.

"What's next?" asked Rani.

Lottie could hardly contain her excitement. "It must be nearly midnight," she said. She looked around at her friends.

"The time has come to begin our search."

Chapter

7

Upstairs

It was, in fact, nine p.m., not midnight, according to the two watches that Zoe always wore. But it was dark enough that it *felt* like midnight, and they'd waited long enough to begin the hunt for the missing cat.

"Right," Lottie ordered, looking at her notebook. "We need to search the school from top to bottom, inside and out."

Mrs Peabody had insisted that the girls would need to be in bed (or in tent) before ten o'clock, so this did not leave Lottie and her team of detectives much time.

"We are going to split up," Lottie told them, opening her notebook. "I have it all planned out. Isabel and Mrs Peabody will come with Pip and me to search the playground and downstairs. Rani, Ava, Zoe and Miss Moody will look for Lady Lovelypaws upstairs."

"Why do we have to split up?" asked Zoe. "And why do I have to be with Ava? She's just going to tell more scary stories."

"People solving a mystery ALWAYS split up," said Lottie crossly. "Haven't you watched *Scooby Doo*? Ghosts are not real, anyway, and besides, you'll have a grown-up with you. Miss Moody won't let Ava scare you."

Zoe reluctantly agreed.

"Hey!" said Rani. "How come you get to have all of the detective stuff? You have to share." It didn't seem fair: Lottie's group had the dog detective *and* most of the supplies Lottie had brought.

"Oh, ALL RIGHT," said Lottie. "Here, you take some rope and the camera." Lottie handed Rani the ancient camera, which had been her dad's when he was a little boy, and both parties set off on tiptoe.

"And remember," called Lottie as they went. "No lights on! We don't want to frighten Lady Lovelypaws away!"

"What about frightening me away?" asked Zoe. "Do we want to do that?"

"We definitely got the scarier bit of the school," Rani whispered to Ava and Zoe as they made their way up to the first floor.

"It's so quiet," whispered Zoe. "It's never this quiet during the day." She shone her torch in every corner, in case Lady Lovelypaws was hiding there. Or in case something else was.

"QUACK! QUACK! QUACK!"

"Ahhhhh!" screamed Zoe, Ava and Rani

together. Zoe jumped into Ava's arms.

"Sorry," said Miss Moody. "I've got a message." She frowned at her phone in the darkness. "Oh dear. I need to call my flatmate. She's lost her keys. Will you be OK for a bit, girls?" Miss Moody dashed back down the staircase.

"She probably doesn't even have a flatmate," said Zoe. "She's scared!"

"Come on," said Rani. "Let's hurry up and get this over with so we can have our midnight feast."

At the top of the stairs, they paused outside the door to the Year Three classroom. It was closed. They all stared at the doorknob.

They listened for scratching.

"Come on," said Ava finally. "It was just a story."

"So you don't believe in ghosts, either?" asked Rani.

"Of course I believe in ghosts," replied Ava.

"But I made that story up. There are no ghosts in the Year Three classroom. Ghosts like scarier places, like attics and cupboards."

Zoe and Rani gulped together. They pushed open the door to the Year Three classroom.

Ava was right: there were no ghosts in Year Three. All was quiet. Through the windows they could see Crabtree Park. In the dim glow of the street lamps, a few dogs were getting their last evening walks.

There was no trace of Lady Lovelypaws anywhere.

Together the three searched the Years Four, Five and Six classrooms. In Year Six they had a good snoop round, to see what the school's eldest girls got up to. The empty desks seemed *a bit* ghostly without their occupants, but there were no *actual* ghosts present, nor were there any cats. Rani took a few photos with Lottie's camera so that they would remember what

Year Six looked like, and then they moved on.

"What's behind there?" asked Rani, pointing to a narrow door at the end of the corridor.

"I don't know," said Ava. "Maybe it's a cupboard?"

"Or an attic," whispered Zoe.

The three of them stood there, frozen.

"You like ghosts," Zoe finally told Ava. "You go first."

"But there could be spiders in there," said Ava. "Or bats or rats."

"I'm not afraid of spiders," said Rani, helpfully. "I'll go first, but if there are ghosts I get to be the first one out."

That seemed fair. Rani opened the door, which creaked like it hadn't been used in ages. The girls found that it did lead to a small cupboard, which was empty except for a wooden ladder covered in cobwebs. It led up through a large hole in the ceiling.

"It's a cupboard AND an attic," Ava told Zoe, as Rani began climbing. "Definitely full of ghosts!"

"Wow," gasped Rani, as first her torch and then her feet disappeared through the hole. "You have to see this!"

With sweaty palms and hearts racing, Ava and Zoe followed her.

When they were all in the attic, their torches lit up the treasures around them. The attic was packed full of hundreds of years of Crabtree School history. Big dusty blackboards, trunks of old-fashioned dresses, piles of old toys and stacks and stacks of musty old textbooks lined the floor and walls.

"Look," said Rani, pointing to an old-fashioned machine with a big horn coming out of it. "That's a gramophone. They used it to listen to music in the olden days! I saw one in a museum."

Zoe got down on her knees to inspect some black-and-white photographs of girls in long skirts. None of them were smiling, which seemed sad. Then she flipped through an old lesson book. *Eliza Smith, 1872*, read the name written on the inside cover. Eliza Smith had good handwriting.

Rani looked through the dusty dresses. She put on a wide hat with a net that covered her face.

"Look at this," said Ava, picking up a small bundle. Rani shone her torch on it. Cradled in Ava's arms was a doll, wearing a grey lacy dress that must have once been white. The doll had golden curls that felt like real hair, and her head was made of china. Ava tipped the doll forward and her glassy eyes opened.

"She's a bit scary," Rani said. "Are those teeth?"

Zoe came in for a closer look. "They are

teeth!" she said. "They look like fangs."

Ava set the doll carefully back in its rusty metal buggy, but none of them could stop staring at its teeth. They were properly scary.

"We should take some photos," Ava told Rani nervously. "Lottie and Isabel will be sad they missed this!"

But just as the camera made its first click, the legs gave out on the ancient doll's buggy and it crashed to the ground.

"What was that?!" shrieked Rani.

"Heeeellllppppp!" screamed Zoe at the top of her lungs. "Help! Somebody help us!" Zoe was hysterical.

"Shhhhhhhh!" whispered Ava, as the three of them huddled together. "It's OK! It was just the doll's buggy."

"We broke it," said Rani sadly. "I hope the doll doesn't get angry." They spent ages trying to mend the doll's buggy but it kept coming apart in their hands.

Then there was a small sound.

"What is that?" said Rani, as softly as she could.

"It sounds like scratching," said Zoe.

Zoe was right; it was scratching. It was coming from the back of the attic, and it was getting louder.

"On the count of three," whispered Ava, "we'll all run to the ladder at once. Rani goes down first."

"One... Two..."

Chapter

Downstairs

"You've definitely left us the scariest bit of the school to investigate," Isabel told Lottie as soon as the others had gone upstairs. The two of them and Mrs Peabody were dragging Pip along the edge of the playground. They had agreed to start their search outside.

"Here, Lady Lovelypaws," called Lottie. "Here, kitty-kitty-kitty. . ."

"Stop saying that!" cried Isabel. "Say anything but that!"

"Meooowwww," called Mrs Peabody into the dark woods that surrounded the playground.

She sounded so much like a real cat that Pip went over to sniff her. When he was sure that she was a human, he lay down at her feet.

Then there was a noise in the woods.

"W-w-what w-w-was that?" Isabel said, trembling. They all stood listening. Even Pip's ears were standing to attention. He got to his feet rather quickly and looked into the darkness.

"Twit-twoo," hooted an owl.

"Just an owl, nothing to be afraid of, girls," Mrs Peabody said. She looked terribly nervous.

"Woof!" barked Pip suddenly. Lottie was really scared then, for she had never heard Pip bark before. She held his lead tightly.

A pair of glowing eyes peered out at them from the darkness of the bushes.

"Meeeooowww?" said Mrs Peabody desperately, as Lottie and Isabel grabbed hold of each other. "Lady Lovelypaws?"

They all gasped in fright as a fox dashed

out of the woods, jumped over the slide and disappeared round the side of the school.

"Woof, woof, woof!" barked Pip excitedly.

"Just a fox, then," said Mrs Peabody, when she'd found her voice again. The headmistress got down from the top of the climbing frame, where she had leapt in fear. "That's enough searching the playground, don't you think, girls? Let's go indoors. Quickly. ASAP. I need a cup of tea."

Lottie and Isabel didn't argue. There was no way that Lady Lovelypaws would be out in the playground with scary foxes about.

The humans turned to go inside, but Pip had other ideas. The excitement had made a new dog out of him. He was sniffing along the side of the school in a frenzy.

"Come on, Pip," said Lottie crossly. "There's nothing there. We're going to look inside." Pip howled, another sound that Lottie had never heard him make before. Finally the dog detective allowed himself to be dragged inside.

Mrs Peabody had not recovered from the playground's wildlife. "I must have a cup of tea, girls," she told Lottie and Isabel. "Do you want one?"

"We're seven," Lottie said. "We don't drink tea."

"I'm eight," corrected Isabel. "But I don't drink tea either."

"Sorry, girls," said Mrs Peabody. "Where is my head? Perhaps a hot chocolate?" Mrs Peabody was always giving the Crabtree girls hot chocolates. Mrs Peabody's hot chocolates were yummy. They had pink marshmallows in them. But tonight Isabel and Lottie had a job to do.

"Mrs Peabody," said Lottie. "Don't you want to find Lady Lovelypaws? What about Mrs Snoop? We can't waste any more time!"

"I know!" exclaimed the headmistress, who still had knocking knees and trembling hands. "But I really, really, *really* need a cup of tea. It is a tea emergency." She opened the door and they all trooped back into the school building.

"Carry on without me," she told Lottie, Isabel and Pip. "I will catch you up as soon as I've had my cuppa." The headmistress dashed into her office.

"Oh, Miss Moody, you frightened me!" Lottie and Isabel heard Mrs Peabody cry. "Why are you hiding under my desk? Shove over, make room for me! I'll put the kettle on."

Without their grown-up, Lottie, Isabel and Pip went to search the assembly room. The stage was quiet; the chairs for the audience eerily empty. Pip sniffed at some pieces of yellow brick road from *The Wizard of Oz* whilst Isabel shone her torch around the folds in the heavy velvet curtain.

"Is that her?" she exclaimed, as she caught sight of a white fluffy thing curled up under a dressing table backstage.

Lottie and Pip raced to investigate, but all they found was a puff of white fur on the top of a Santa Claus hat that someone had worn for last year's Christmas play.

"Shame," said Isabel sadly. "I really thought that was her!"

Lottie put the Santa hat on Pip's head, and the downstairs detectives moved on. They searched the Rainbow Room (which had nothing scary about it at all, even late at night), the music room and the kitchen. Then Pip sniffed his way through the lower school classrooms. Everything was dark, quiet and cat-free.

They *even* looked in the Crabtree School Staffroom, which was the special teachers-only room that no students were allowed in, ever. It was filled with old sofas, old paintings and old cups of half-drunk tea.

"Wow!" cried Isabel as they peered through the door.

"What is it? Do you see her?" Lottie pushed in behind Isabel, shining her torch around frantically.

"No, but look! They have bowls of mints in here! And a television!"

"We've looked EVERYWHERE," said Isabel sadly when they'd closed the door on the

staffroom. "I don't think Lady Lovelypaws is going to come out, even if it is night-time!"

"There is one place we haven't looked," said Lottie, when she'd finished writing down about the mints and the TV in her notebook.

"Where?" asked Isabel.

"We haven't looked in the toilets," Lottie told her. "She could be in there."

"Why would a cat be in the toilets?"

"We've got to check EVERYWHERE," Lottie said firmly.

"Fine, then," replied Isabel. "You and Pip go look in the toilets. I'll wait here."

"Pip is a boy," Lottie argued. "He can't go in the girls' toilets. You go and Pip and I will stay here."

"Pip is a dog," said Isabel. "He won't mind if the toilets are for girls. But I'll hold him if you like, whilst you go in."

Isabel and Lottie shone their torches on each

other's faces. They were best friends, and they had a lot in common. For one thing, they both loved reading. Just that very week they had both finished reading the same very famous book. In this famous book, something *properly* scary had happened in the girls' toilets. Something that neither Isabel nor Lottie could forget.

"Go on," said Isabel. "You're the detective."

"No way," said Lottie. "Not on my own."

They both stared at the door to the toilets.

"I am sure," Lottie told Isabel in her most confident voice, "that there are no ghosts or monsters or trolls or anything like that in there. That doesn't happen in real life, only in books."

"Then you go in."

"We'll both go," Lottie decided. "Besides, in *Harry Potter* it was the FIRST floor girls' toilets, and this is the GROUND floor girls' toilets. So it's perfectly safe."

Holding hands once again, they went in.

The lights were off, of course, but the white sinks and walls glowed in the moonlight that shone in through the window.

A sudden movement to their right made them both jump, but it was only their own reflections in the mirror. It was dead silent except for the *click click* of Pip's nails on the tile floor.

"See?" said Lottie. "Nothing to be afraid of. Do you need the loo?"

"No way," said Isabel. Neither did Lottie. Both girls were secretly hoping they wouldn't need the toilet again until tomorrow morning.

They were back out in the hallway when they heard the scream: "Heeeeellllppp!"

Chapter

Downstairs Upstairs

"That sounded like Zoe!" shouted Lottie, as she and Isabel ran towards the sound. "It's coming from upstairs!"

They raced to the front hall. Pip led the way, still wearing the Father Christmas hat. He was sliding all over the slippery marble floor.

"It sounded like it came from *above* the first floor!" said Isabel as they ran. "Could they be on the roof?"

"Quick," shouted Lottie. "Follow me!" She stopped suddenly in front of a huge painting in the stairwell. Isabel ran into the back of her.

Lottie pushed against the painting. There was a creak, and then it swung open like a door. Before Isabel could blink, Lottie was disappearing down a narrow hallway towards a steep set of stairs, Pip galloping alongside her. Isabel followed, too curious to hesitate. The painting slammed shut behind her.

"A secret passage!" cried Isabel as they climbed the stairs. "But were does it lead?"

"To the top of the school!" whispered Lottie. After a short climb they came to a small wooden door. It was locked. Lottie pushed against it. "We can't go any further," she said at last. "I've tried before. I thought for sure the others had found the secret passage." Pip scratched at the door like a wild animal. He was sure too.

"What's that sound?" asked Isabel nervously. "I hear voices. It has to be ghosts! The others couldn't have got in, could they?"

Isabel did not know that there were two

ways into the attic. In fact, until that moment she hadn't even known that Crabtree School *had* an attic.

Lottie had hidden in the secret passage many times. She knew there must be *something* behind that door at the top, but she had never been able to get inside.

"Shhhh," hissed Lottie, putting her ear to the door. "Listen, it sounds like counting!"

"A counting ghost?" said Isabel. She leaned against the door too.

Inside the attic, Ava *was* counting. On the count of three, Ava and Rani and Zoe were going to run away from the terrible scratching they heard.

Outside, the weight of a seven-year-old, an eight-year-old and a very persistent dog proved too much for the old wooden door to withstand. Suddenly the downstairs detectives found themselves crashing into the attic.

After the crash came the loudest screaming ever to be heard under the Crabtree School roof. Then Lottie heard the sounds of frantic scrambling and of things being dropped. The room was filled with strange shadows as torches rolled about on the floor.

"Look!" shouted Isabel. "In the corner! Ghosts!"

Caught in a flash of light were three dusty figures. One was glowing with strange spots. Another was wearing a scary olden-days hat. The third was truly terrifying in a long ghostly dress.

The spooky figures began to run about madly, and so did Isabel. The commotion brought up smoky clouds of dust, which only increased the panic in the attic.

Amid the commotion, Pip merely stood wagging his tail at them all. The ghost-hunting dog detective was not afraid. Neither was his mistress.

"Stop!" said Lottie calmly, picking up a fallen torch. "Ava, Rani, Zoe, it's just us! It's Lottie and Isabel!"

Lottie knew that there was no such thing as ghosts. And anyway, she would recognize Ava's fairy nightdress and Zoe's crazy glow-in-the-dark pyjamas anywhere. Rani's unicorn top was clearly visible in the torchlight.

"It's you," gasped Ava. She looked disappointed not to have seen a real live ghost.

Just then, Mrs Peabody poked her head up from the space in the floor where Zoe, Rani and Ava had climbed up.

"Girls," she said. "You are very brave to look up here, but I think it best if you come down at once. Lady Lovelypaws would never come to the attic. There could be rats and bats and spiders up here." Mrs Peabody trembled at the thought. The cup of tea in her hand wobbled as she went back down the ladder.

The girls hurried down behind her, and, to Lottie's relief, the secret passage remained mostly a secret.

Chapter

S'more Searching

Back on the ground floor, Lottie sat updating the map of Crabtree School in her notebook. She needed to add the first floor cupboard and the attic.

"What should we do now?" asked Isabel, picking up a rumpled sleepover schedule.

Lottie turned to a page in her notebook. It was labelled PLAN B: DO THIS IF WE DON'T FIND LADY LOVELYPAWS WHEN WE SEARCH. Lottie had a plan for everything.

"Now," said Lottie confidently, "we need to make it really dark. No torches or anything.

Then we climb into the tent and wait for Lady Lovelypaws to come to us." Lottie opened up a tin of cat food and set out the toy mice.

"That doesn't sound very fun," said Rani. "What about the midnight feast? Eww, that cat food stinks."

"We'll have the midnight feast later," Lottie told her. "After we find Lady Lovelypaws."

Isabel yawned. "What if we fall asleep first?"

"Oh, fine!" said Lottie. Her eyes were beginning to feel as heavy as Pip's looked. They all went off to the kitchen to have a look and wake themselves up a bit.

"There's nothing here," said Rani sadly. It was true; the Crabtree cupboards were bare. All the food from last week had been eaten up, and the food for next week's school lunches hadn't arrived yet.

"Do you have anything in your suitcase, Lottie?" asked Ava hopefully. But it turned out that food was the one thing Lottie *hadn't* brought.

"How about some green sweeties?" offered Miss Moody kindly. "I've been saving them for the last day of term because they are my favourite, but you can have them."

At least one mystery had been solved. Lottie updated SUBJECT: MISS MOODY in her notebook, and put a big tick in the CASE SOLVED? box.

But a few green sweeties would make a sorry midnight feast. Rani smiled weakly at the Year Three teacher. Miss Moody meant well but—

"What's going on in here? Who's in my kitchen?" Mrs Crunch appeared in the doorway. Colonel Crunch was behind her, holding a lantern. They had come all the way from their cottage.

"Mrs Crunch, do you have anything we could eat for our midnight feast?" asked Rani. "Something delicious?"

They all looked at the dinner lady with pleading eyes.

"Pretty please?" asked Isabel.

"I have just the thing," replied Mrs Crunch, reaching for a package of marshmallows hidden on a high shelf. "But Colonel Crunch will have to build us a fire."

The whole Crabtree sleepover crowd stood round a crackling campfire on the edge of the playground. Colonel Crunch toasted a marshmallow on a stick. When it was warm and gooey and just a little bit burnt, Mrs Crunch smooshed it between two chocolate digestives.

"It's called a s'more," Colonel Crunch explained, handing it to Isabel. "Because you always want some more."

"It's the best thing I've ever tasted," said Isabel, as Lottie began a notebook entry titled HOW TO MAKE A S'MORE.

"I can't wait to tell my brothers," smiled Rani. They took turns roasting marshmallows and licking their sticky fingers. They told the grown-ups all about their adventure in the attic, and how they had mistaken each other for ghosts.

"I'm sorry to have missed it, girls," said Mrs Peabody. She and Miss Moody were a bit embarrassed about what fraidy-cats they had been.

"Don't worry," said Rani. "I took lots of photos. Only I hope I didn't break your camera, Lottie. I dropped it on the floor when I thought ghosts were chasing us! But I can't get the photos I took to show up now."

"It's an olden-days camera," Lottie explained. "It has film that you have to take to get printed into photos. My mum will do it for us."

As she was finishing her third s'more, Lottie noticed the headmistress gazing sadly into the fire.

"We'll find her, Mrs Peabody," said Lottie bravely. She gave Mrs Peabody a hug. "We'll stay up all night if we have to."

As they gazed into the fire, neither the headmistress nor Lottie noticed the statue-like face that was peering over the playground fence. For Lottie was not the only one who was determined to solve The Case of the Missing Cat.

"Here, kitty-kitty-kitty," called Mrs Snoop softly as she crept round the side of the school.

Mrs Snoop was not giving up, either.

Chapter

The Rescuers

It is actually quite difficult to stay up *all* night. After they'd sent the grown-ups off to bed, the girls zipped themselves into their sleeping bags to begin the wait for Lady Lovelypaws. They flipped over Isabel's sign so that it read: **DETECTIVES SLEEPING**, just in case Lady Lovelypaws could read. Then they used Zoe's watches, which glowed in the dark like her pyjamas, to keep track of the time.

Isabel was the first to fall asleep. By half past ten, she was snoozing peacefully on her back. Her robe and bunny slippers were bundled neatly beside her.

By eleven o'clock, Ava was off to dreamland. At her feet, the five dolls slept too, in their little tent.

Rani wasn't far behind Ava. Her mouth was still smeared with chocolate from their midnight feast, and she was chewing in her sleep. Lottie thought she was probably dreaming of more s'mores.

Just after eleven-thirty p.m., Zoe's eyes closed and her head dropped on to her hands. After that, Lottie couldn't see her watches anymore.

Finally, some time before dawn, Lottie went to sleep too. Her notebook was tucked under her pillow and Pip lay curled up beside her.

Lottie dreamt she was on a bouncy castle. She was jumping and falling and getting pushed all around. She woke up and realized that someone had actually been shaking her, trying to wake her up.

"She's shrunk!" hissed Rani. "Someone has shrunk Lady Lovelypaws!" Lottie put on her glasses to find Rani holding a tiny ball of white fur. It was a cat. This cat looked just like Lady Lovelypaws. Only it was a LOT smaller. "I found her in my trainer!" said Rani.

"How? What?" Lottie wriggled out of her sleeping bag. She looked down at Pip, who was still asleep. All that investigating had worn him out. Snuggled in between his paws was another miniature Lady Lovelypaws.

Rani saw it too. "Another one! Kittens!"

There was a third baby Lady Lovelypaws asleep in Ava's doll tent, and one in Isabel's bunny slipper. A fifth was curled up in Zoe's wavy hair.

As the rest of the girls struggled awake, there came the sound of a desperate meow. Someone was in real trouble. There were only a few creatures in Crabtree School that could make a meow like that.

The five human detectives and their dog sprang from the tent, leaving the tiny Lady Lovelypawses behind them.

"Mrs Peabody?" shouted Lottie, as they threw open her office door. "Are you OK?"

The headmistress was asleep on top of her desk, clutching the photo of Lady Lovelypaws. The meow had not come from her. Across from Mrs Peabody, Miss Moody snored away in a chair. The five friends tucked Mrs Peabody's blanket around her and backed out of the office. They tiptoed back to their tent.

They stood looking at the kittens, who had now crawled out on to the quilt.

"How can there be kittens but still no Lady Lovelypaws?" asked Isabel.

Then they heard another meow. Pip jumped to his feet. "Follow that dog!" shouted Lottie as Pip headed for the playground.

"We've already looked out here," said Ava. "Where could she have been hiding?" Pip went to the side of the school. He scratched and dug against the bricks, but there was nothing there.

Lottie got down on her hands and knees and felt along the bottom of the school's red brick wall.

"A hole!" she cried. "Quick, get me a torch!"

There, in a dark cavern under Crabtree School, Lady Lovelypaws crouched over one last tiny version of herself. But this kitten's leg had got stuck between two bits of brick in the back of the little cave. Holding the kitten in her mouth by the back of its neck, Lady Lovelypaws tugged and tugged, but she couldn't get the kitten's leg out.

"Quick, get a grown-up!" cried Isabel. "The kitten is going to get hurt!"

"A grown-up won't fit in there," said Ava.

"The hole is too small."

"Let me try!" said Lottie. She got down on her stomach and slithered into the hole. Once she got close to the kitten, Lottie ever-so-gently lifted its tiny foot out of the crack in the bricks.

Lady Lovelypaws purred and purred. She picked up the kitten in her mouth again.

"Let's get out of here," Lottie told the mummy cat. "I don't want Colonel Crunch seeing us and boarding up this hole. It's a perfect hiding place!"

Lady Lovelypaws smiled in agreement.

Chapter

A Cracking Good Time Was Had by All

"Six beautiful babies!" cried Mrs Peabody. She stood beaming at the kittens, a cup of tea in her hand.

"So that's where you've been," she said to Lady Lovelypaws. "Off looking after your kittens! I've missed you so."

Lady Lovelypaws smiled up at the headmistress and rubbed against her legs.

"I think," said Rani, watching the kittens play in the doll tent, "that maybe Lady Lovelypaws meant to give each of us a kitten? When we woke up, we each had one. There was one in my trainer, one was in Zoe's hair..."

"I'm certain she did," replied the headmistress. "You are very brave, girls, and you saved the day. Who better to look after Lady Lovelypaws's children than you five? Of course, we'll have to ask your parents, but I'm sure it will be fine." Mrs Peabody couldn't believe anyone would turn down the chance to have their very own Lady Lovelypaws.

A tent, ghost stories, s'mores and now a kitten as a going-home present: Lottie thought that this surely must be the best sleepover in the history of the world.

"But wait," said Zoe, who had already decided to call her kitten Eliza. "There are six kittens. Who will take the last one? The poor little one that got stuck?"

Mrs Peabody said Crabtree School already had a cat, and needed only one. Miss Moody had a dog at home that wasn't quite as friendly as Pip. The Crunches were far too busy keeping up with the Crabtree girls to look after a cat.

"But what will happen to her?" insisted Lottie. "She needs a good home!"

"We'll sort it out, girls," said Mrs Peabody. "First, let's have some breakfast."

"That poor little guy will be sad," said Ava, whose own kitten was called Zinkelflop. (Ava was convinced that aliens had something to do with all this excitement.) "All of her friends have lovely homes to go to, but she doesn't."

They were just tucking into Mrs Crunch's delicious blueberry pancakes when there was a bang at the front door.

"Who would be visiting on a Saturday morning?" wondered Mrs Peabody aloud. Shortly after she went to see who it was, they heard Mrs Snoop's voice in the hall.

"What is SHE doing here?" shrieked Rani. "Quick! Hide the kittens!" They stashed two kittens in Isabel's robe pockets, one under Lottie's black hat, one between two pancakes and one under an overturned teacup. Lady Lovelypaws scurried under a table. But where was the last kitten?

"I was hoping someone would be here," Mrs Snoop was saying to Mrs Peabody as they came in. "We like to search the schools for animals on the weekends, when no children are about." Mrs Snoop stopped when she saw the pancake breakfast.

"What's this?" she asked, her face as stony as ever. "Why are there children here?"

Mrs Snoop knew the answer to this of course, because she had seen the girls around the campfire the night before, but she couldn't very well let on that she had been spying.

As Mrs Peabody and the five friends tried desperately to think of what to say, Isabel's kitten, which she had named Mabel, was crawling out from under the pancakes.

Lottie saw the teacup with Rani's kitten under it move across the table. Rani's kitten was called Girl, because Rani was happy that it was one.

The kitten under her hat was nibbling on Lottie's ear, and it was hard not to giggle. Lottie's kitten was called Sweetie.

"I shall have a good look round now," said Mrs Snoop. "I hope that you have listened to my warning, Mrs Peabody. I'm sure you know better than to break rule four thousand, three hundred and twenty-one aga— Ahhhhh!"

A kitten was wobbling across the floor towards Mrs Snoop's feet.

"What is the meaning of THIS?" cried Mrs Snoop. The woman was so shocked that Lottie thought she saw Mrs Snoop's face move the tiniest bit. "What *dirty, smelly,* FEROCIOUS creature is this?"

Everyone knows that kittens are not dirty, or smelly, or ferocious. They are snuggly and fluffy and quite possibly the cutest things on the planet. Kittens are not afraid of grouchy old ladies, either. Lady Lovelypaws's tiniest baby trotted right up to Mrs Snoop's shoe.

"It's attacking me!" screamed Mrs Snoop. "Get it AWAY! Call the police!" Her lips were moving a bit as she shouted.

As they watched, the kitten climbed right up Mrs Snoop's shoe. It began licking her ankle.

"OH HELLLLPPP!" shrieked Mrs Snoop. "It's eating me alive! It's . . . aah – hee hee. Ha ha. Hee hee – that tickles!" Mrs Snoop's eyebrows went up in surprise. There was a small cracking sound as her stony skin began to move.

"Go on," said Lottie. "Pick him up. He won't hurt you!"

Mrs Snoop bent over. She looked at the tiny kitten rubbing against her. He liked her soft, puffy ankles. He was purring.

Mrs Snoop reached out a bony finger to touch the fluffy white fur. She began to stroke the kitten. He chewed at her shoelace.

Ever so slowly, Mrs Snoop picked up the ball of white fur with two hands and held him up in front of her face. There were little cracks showing where her forehead had moved.

There was a gasp all round as the kitten batted Mrs Snoop's nose with his little paw. They all waited to see what would happen next.

Mrs Snoop's lips twitched. Her cheeks quivered. With a loud creaking, cracking, crumbling sound, her stony face broke into a smile.

Mrs Snoop's smile wasn't just a small one. It was the kind you make with your whole face. Lottie thought that she looked like the happiest person in the world just then. Which was saying a lot, considering Mrs Snoop was surrounded by five little girls who'd just had a sleepover AND been given a kitten.

Mrs Snoop fed her kitten milk with a tiny spoon as the girls finished their breakfast and packed up Lottie's tent. Whilst they waved goodbye to Mrs Peabody and Lady Lovelypaws, they saw Mrs Snoop tucking the kitten gently into the pocket of her grey coat. She was still smiling.

They never heard another word about SCAT again, though some weeks later Mrs Peabody did receive a note from Mrs Snoop, asking if she could bring the kitten, who was now called Rocky, to the Crabtree School Pet Parade in the spring.

There were a few exclamations of "You've brought home a WHAT?" from the mummies and daddies later that morning, but with lots of convincing and googolplex pleases, the other five kittens found loving homes with Zoe, Rani, Isabel, Ava and Lottie. Pip and Sweetie became the best of friends and took long naps snuggled up together.

Lady Lovelypaws lived at Crabtree School for the rest of her nine lives, and over the years she had many more kittens that brought many more smiles to many more faces. Kittens will do that.

Chapter

Epilogue, Which Means
What Happened Later

Lottie, Ava, Isabel, Zoe and Rani were sat in Lottie's hideout in a secret location somewhere in Lottie's garden. In Lottie's hand was an envelope, and in this envelope were the photographs from the greatest sleepover in the history of the world.

"My mum has just got them back from the olden-days camera place!" said Lottie excitedly. Huddled together, the friends began to look through the pictures.

There was a photo of the tent, with all of their sleepover supplies.

There was one of Ava's face, lit by a torch, looking delighted to be terrifying them all.

There was one featuring Mrs Peabody in her robe and curlers, and Miss Moody in her sheep pyjamas.

There were loads of pictures of the Year Six classroom, and one of the creepy doll in the attic.

Looking through the pictures felt like they were at the sleepover all over again. Eventually they came to the last photograph.

"I don't remember taking that one," said Rani. "Do you, Lottie?" Lottie did not.

The picture was of the attic. It was a bit blurry, and quite dark.

"That must have been when you dropped the camera, Rani," said Lottie. They leaned in for a closer look.

They could see Rani's sparkly knees, but most of the photo was of Ava, in her long white nightdress. At her feet, there was a small white cloud. It looked a little like a cat, except they could see right through it to the broken doll's buggy behind.

"What's that?" asked Rani, pointing.

They stared.

"It looks like—" stuttered Isabel.

"I knew it!" said Ava.

"But it can't be," replied Zoe.

"It has to be," said Lottie. "We have proof." She tucked the photo into her purple notebook.

They would need to do more investigating.

Carry on reading
for lots more
Crabtree School
fun!

ALL ABOUT ME

MY FULL NAME: Charlotte Christina Lewis, aka: Lottie, Charlie, Doodles

WHERE I LIVE: 22lb Birchwood Lane

WHAT MY ROOM LOOKS LIKE: It looks normal, but it has **LOTS** of great hiding places, including a secret passage from under my bed to under my desk.

WHO IS IN MY FAMILY: There is my mummy, who is called Francesca Lewis and gets lots of parking tickets. Also my dad, who is called John Lewis like the shop and is not good at barbecuing. Last is my sister, Lola Lewis, who is four years old and last week coloured on our sofa with a marker pen.

MY PETS: I have a dog called Pip Lewis who snores a lot. He will not eat the regular kind of dog food, only the really fancy kind.

MY BEST FRIEND(S): My best friend is Isabel. She is good at crafts and has a shoebox as her secret hiding place.

WHAT I LOVE TO DO: I love to go to the movies and watch people. I like to watch people in real life, too. And I love solving mysteries!

WHAT MAKES ME CROSS: When grown-ups think kids don't know what they are talking about it makes me VERY cross. I always know what everyone is talking about!

WHAT I AM MOST AFRAID OF: Vampire bats, because they are real animals that really exist. And also trolls. Trolls are scary.

WHAT I COLLECT: Clues!

MY SECRET HIDING PLACE: No way am I
answering that! It's a SECRET!

HOW TO BE A GOOD SPY
by Lottie

1)   Always be on the lookout for good hiding places! Don t choose hot places, cold places, smelly places or places where a grown-up might see you and make you help tidy up/set the table/practise piano.

2)   Keep your notebook with you at all times. It can go in your sock, in your pocket, in your shoe or even in your ponytail. But keep it close, and away from little sisters.

3)   Write down EVERYTHING. You never know what might be important for solving a mystery someday! But do remember the Golden Rule of Spying:

Never write anything mean about anyone. Never. Because a truly good spy is a kind one!

THE CASE OF THE MISSING CAT HAS EVERYTHING FROM A KOOKY OLD DOG TO LITTLE FLUFFY KITTENS, BUT WHICH ANIMAL ARE YOU? TAKE THE QUIZ TO FIND OUT!

1. What's your bedroom like?
a. Neat and tidy
b. Pretty messy, but bright
c. Cosy and comfy
d. Full of games and stuff
e. Really grown-up

2. Choose a fun activity:
a. Something crafty
b. Swimming
c. Playing hide-and-seek
d. Going to the funfair
e. Dressing up

3. What word describes you best?

a. Curious

b. Loyal

c. Kind

d. Energetic

e. Strong

4. What's your favourite food?

a. Fish fingers

b. Hamburger

c. Cake

d. Crisps

e. Popcorn

5. What's your favourite colour?

a. Green

b. Red

c. Orange

d. Silver

e. Blue

6. What's your favourite school activity?

a. Story time

b. Play time

c. Lunch time

d. Drama

e. PE

7. What do you like to do with your friends?

a. Put on a play

b. Run around outside

c. Make dens and forts

d. Dance

e. Play make-believe

8. What's your favourite season?

a. Summer

b. Spring

c. Autumn

d. Winter

e. You like them all!

Mostly As: A Cat!

You're a regular Lady Lovelypaws! You love school and you're curious about new things and ideas. Your room is always neat and tidy, and your favourite thing to do is curl up in bed with a good book. You're never in a rush and you like to do things at your own pace — gently and gracefully.

Mostly Bs: A Dog!

You're like Pip, only with a lot more energy! You love running around outside more than anything and are always looking for a fun new game to play with your friends. You can be a bit messy (sorry, Mum!), but that's because you have so many fun things to do. Once you're friends with someone they're a friend forever.

Mostly Cs: A Rabbit!

You'd be right at home in Isabel's rabbit hutch!

You're really easy-going and extremely kind to everyone you meet – you love making other people happy. You always have a fun plan for what to do on a play date or during break, and everyone always has a good time when you are in charge.

Mostly Ds: A Hamster!

You're so energetic no one can pin you down for more than second. You love to dance and go to parties with your friends, and you are brilliant at doing tricks. Sitting still is far too boring for you, but when you aren't running about, you're the most caring creature around. You are very good at looking after younger children, which is lucky because, at Crabtree School, you live in the Reception classroom!

Mostly Es: A Horse!

You're the pony every Crabtree girl dreams of!

You love going to new places and exploring – you're always up for an adventure or learning something new. You're sometimes shy when you meet new people, but when you're with your best friends you're fun, loyal and brave, no matter what.

CRABTREE SCHOOL

Collect all the Crabtree School books!

Lauren Pearson

CRABTREE SCHOOL

Year Two Forever and Ever

Lauren Pearson

CRABTREE SCHOOL

Best Friends for Never

Lauren Pearson

CRABTREE SCHOOL

The Girl Who Stole the World

Lauren Pearson

CRABTREE SCHOOL

The Case of the Missing Cat

Win a family set of scooters!

To celebrate the brilliant Crabtree School series we've got four brand new Micro Scooters® to give away! The lucky winner will also receive a signed set of four Crabtree School books.

Scooting as a family is the perfect way to spend quality time together; you can travel in style and then snuggle down at story time with the Crabtree School gang. Ideal for lots of family fun, you won't want to miss out on this amazing prize!

Visit **www.crabtreeschool.com** to enter the free competition before it closes at midnight on 31st December 2015.

Good luck!

*T&Cs apply – visit **www.crabtreeschool.com** for full details

www.micro-scooters.co.uk